Judith Vigna

Gregory's Stitches

Gregorio y sus puntos

The Little Boy Who Loved Dirt
and Almost Became a Superslob

Couldn't We Have a Turtle Instead?

Everyone Goes as a Pumpkin

Story and Pictures by Judith Vigna

Albert Whitman & Company, Chicago

©1977 by Judith Vigna
Published simultaneously in Canada
by George J. McLeod, Limited, Toronto
All rights reserved. Printed in the U.S.A.

Library of Congress Cataloging in Publication Data

Vigna, Judith.
  Everyone goes as a pumpkin.

  (Self-starter books)
  SUMMARY: When Emily loses her beautiful costume,
she must decide what to be for the Halloween party.
  [1.   Halloween—Fiction]   I.   Title.
PZ7.V67Ev   [E]   77-14254
ISBN 0-8075-2186-8

Emily had the best Halloween costume
of all. It was gold and glittery and absolutely
gorgeous.

It would make her look like
someone from a storybook
at the party, somebody special.

It might even win her a prize.

The day of the party,
Emily took her costume
to show her grandmother.

On the bus,
she put the box
carefully on the seat
beside her.

Then an
awful thing
happened.

When she got to her stop,
the box was gone!

She ran all the way to
her grandmother's and
told her the terrible news.

"It's not so bad," said her grandmother.
"We can make you another costume.
Why don't you go as a pumpkin?
All we need is paper and paint.
We can make you a pumpkin costume
in no time."

"No," sobbed Emily, "I don't want to go as a pumpkin. *Everyone* goes as a pumpkin!"

"A skeleton, then? The store is still open. Why don't we go out and buy you a skeleton costume?"

"I don't want to be an ugly skeleton.
I want to be *beautiful*."

"Well, then," her grandmother said,
"why don't you go as yourself?"

Emily thought about that. But she
shook her head. "No. Everybody has
to *be* someone."

"You're someone, Emily. You're *you*."
And Emily thought about that, too.

So she dried her eyes,
kissed her grandmother...

...and went to the party.

And after a while, she forgot
all about her beautiful costume—

—because just being Emily
was the most fun of all.